CW00432495

FLOODIN' OUT

REAL ESTATE RESCUE COZY MYSTERIES, BOOK 7

PATTI BENNING

SUMMER PRESCOTT BOOKS PUBLISHING

CHAPTER ONE

Flora Abner had been planning to sleep in that Saturday morning, but a loud yowl, a crash, and the sudden influx of morning light made her sit bolt upright in bed at the tender hour of just seven o'clock.

"Amaretto! What's gotten into you?"

Her fluffy white Persian cat delicately untangled herself from the curtain that was now on the floor, along with the curtain rod. The cat must have tried climbing the sheer fabric, probably in a mad attempt to catch a bird that flew by on the other side of the window.

"You're going feral," Flora moaned and she flopped back down and pulled a pillow over her face. The damage had been done, though. There was no going back to sleep, not after the shot of adrenaline that brought her to wakefulness.

A dip on the bed told her the cat had jumped up. Soon, small paws started kneading her rib cage. Without looking, she extended her hand to stroke the cat's spine. Amaretto had grown up as a lazy, spoiled apartment cat. Now that they lived on a few rural acres in the small town of Warbler, Kentucky, the cat had discovered a wild streak Flora didn't know she had.

"Fine, I'm getting up," she grumbled when the cat butted her head into her hand. "You're not getting breakfast this early, though. If we start that, you're just going to keep waking me up at seven every day. You can wait until your regular time."

She got out of bed and opened her door, shuffling out into the living room. It was too early for the sun to be fully up, but gray dawn light streamed in through the window behind the couch. The grassy field across the road from her house looked quiet and peaceful, with mist filling the space before the trees began.

There was something quiet and almost magical about early mornings out in the countryside. Her annoyance with Amaretto faded quickly, though she had to fight back a yawn as she shuffled out of the living room and down the hall to the first-floor bathroom.

She was still sleeping in the tiny third bedroom on the first floor that she had claimed as her own when she first moved into the house. Now that both of the upstairs bedrooms had been repainted and their hardwood floors had been refinished, she knew she should move her own bedroom up there soon. With a full bath and more space, it would serve to make her mornings easier. Plus, she would need all of her things out of the small room in order to finally start renovating it. She had made a lot of progress on her fixer-upper house in the months since she had moved here, but it was still far from being ready to flip and sell.

She pushed the bathroom door fully open, not bothering to turn on the lights as she stepped inside. Her foot splashed into a puddle of water, and she jumped back with a yelp, slapping blindly at the wall for the light switch. She managed to hit both it, and the switch for the fan, which choked and scraped its way to life. Her distracted mind made a note to replace it, but then all of her attention was focused on the horror awaiting her in her bathroom.

The floor was flooded. Water covered every inch

of it and was still dripping out of the cabinet beneath the sink. The flood was beginning to creep into the hallway, darkening the old, dry floorboards she had been putting off refinishing.

A wordless noise of horror croaked out of her mouth. She hadn't left the sink on, so a pipe must be leaking, and it was getting worse by the minute.

"Okay," she said out loud, trying to calm her panic. "I need to think. The longer I wait, the worse this is going to get. I just... I need to turn the water off. Yeah." She stood there for a second longer, slowly realizing that she had no idea where the water shut off was.

"I need Grady," she decided after a moment. She rushed back into the bedroom, passing Amaretto where she was perched on the back of the couch, looking out the window. The cat's rude early-morning awakening was a blessing in disguise, because this mess would be even worse if she had slept in for another couple of hours like she was planning.

She grabbed her phone from where she had left it on the nightstand and, with a glance at the time, quickly dialed Grady's number. He didn't have a cell phone, so the only way to contact him was by calling his landline number. He had to be at the hardware store soon to open it by eight, but it was still early and he didn't live very far away, so she thought he would probably both be awake, and still at home.

She felt a rush of relief when he answered with a concerned, "Flora?"

"It's an emergency," she said. "Sort of. One of the pipes in the bathroom is leaking and there is water everywhere. How do I shut it off?"

"Go down to your water heater in the basement," he said. "There should be a lever –"

"Hold on, need to grab the flashlight. Give me two seconds."

She hurried to the basement door, which was in the hallway between the kitchen and the living room, and pulled it open, taking a flashlight down from the shelf just inside of it. She flicked the switch for the single, dim bulb then started down the stairs.

The dim bulb wasn't enough to illuminate every corner of the basement. If she was being honest with herself, she didn't like the basement very much. It was dark and dusty, and *creepy*. She didn't believe in ghosts, but if her house *had* a ghost, this was where it would be.

"All right, I'm at the water heater," she said. "Now what?"

"There should be a lever on one of the pipes going into it. The handle might be red or yellow–"

"I see it. Should I pull it?"

"Yes. That should be the water shut off for your house."

She pulled the lever, making sure it was fully closed. Then she turned and rushed back upstairs, splashed into the bathroom, and pulled open the cupboard doors. One of the pipes underneath the sink was wet and dripping, but it wasn't actively leaking anymore.

"That worked," she said, breathing a sigh of relief. "Thank you so much."

"Do you know where the leak is coming from?"

"Well, the joint on one of the pipes is corroded. Underneath that joint everything is wet. I'm guessing it came from there. Do you think I should call someone? Is this something I can fix myself?"

"It should be an easy enough fix," he said. "You'll need some supplies. I'll pick some stuff up while I'm at work, and come over to help you with it after the hardware store closes. If it's not very busy, I'll ask Mr. Brant if I can leave early so you don't have to spend all day without any running water. I'll call you either way and let you know."

"Thank you," she said with feeling. "You are a lifesaver, Grady."

She said her goodbyes to him, then snapped a quick picture of the mess in her bathroom to send to Violet along with the message, *Might have to delay our plans, had a house related emergency this morning.*

They had been planning to meet for brunch and do some shopping together. Even though Flora didn't have strict working hours, she still tried to take one day a week completely off from working on the house. She needed the time to have fun guilt free, and being locked up in her house all day, every day could feel suffocating.

Once that was done, she started pulling everything out from under the sink. The towels she kept under there were soaking wet, and all of her extra toilet paper was destroyed. Luckily she had some more towels upstairs, and some that were sitting in the dryer, freshly washed. She would have to get everything dried off as quickly as possible to hopefully avoid any water damage to the floor.

Her phone buzzed with an incoming text message and she paused to read it. *Oh no. Do you want help cleaning it? I can grab some coffees and head over.*

I'd kill for a latte right now, but don't feel like you

have to help. I'm mostly just going to be drying every-thing off.

Violet responded almost as soon as she had sent the message saying, *I'll be there in 20 minutes!*

Feeling a little better now that the emergency was under control and she would probably end up still having a nice day with her friend, she took the sopping wet towels outside to wring them out, then hung them over the porch railing to dry before going back in to take the towels from the upstairs bathroom and start drying everything.

Half an hour later, and the bathroom was almost dry. She was keeping an ear out for the sound of Violet's car pulling up, but something must have held her friend up. When her phone rang, she jumped to answer it. It was from the hardware store – it would be Grady calling to let her know whether or not he would be able to get off work early.

"Hello?" she said, putting the call on speaker so she could continue to mop up the rest of the water under the sink.

"Hey," Grady said. "I don't know if I'll be able to get off early today. My boss still isn't here. I'll talk to him about it when he comes in, though. Could you get a measurement of the pipes for me? What are they made out of? Usually it's PVC or copper. It might be red or blue pex piping if it's had work done recently."

"It's copper," she said. "And I can try to measure it, let me go find a measuring tape."

She got the information Grady needed, and ended the call with him so she could check for text messages from Violet. She frowned, getting a little worried. It had been almost forty minutes since her friend's text message, and it wasn't like Violet to be late.

Once she was done in the bathroom, she went into the kitchen to feed Amaretto breakfast, though she forewent making herself her normal morning cup of coffee since Violet said she was bringing some over. She was going to have to do a load of laundry today, since all of her towels were wet, and she couldn't take her usual morning shower since she didn't have any water. It was a bad start to the day, but she hoped things would improve soon.

Her phone rang again, interrupting her reverie. She saw Violet's name on the caller ID and was quick to press the button to accept the call.

"Hey. Everything all right?"

When her friend answered, her voice was choked with tears. "I need you to come pick me up. I'm on the main road between your house and town, about a mile away from that cemetery."

Worry surged through Flora. "What happened?"

"I… I hit someone with my car. He's dead. The police are here. My car is totaled and they said I need to get a ride."

Flora's stomach dropped. "I'll be right there," she promised, then ran towards her front door.

CHAPTER TWO

Flora was so flustered she almost forgot to grab her purse on her way out. She slammed the door behind her without even pausing to lock it, and got into her truck, glad that she had finally fixed the driveway because she backed out so quickly, the old potholes probably would have wrecked her suspension.

She took off down the dirt road, spitting gravel behind her, and turned onto the main road that led into town. It was a long, country road full of twists and turns. She felt sick at heart knowing that Violet had hit someone. Someone had lost their life, and her friend's life would never be the same. Horrible guilt gnawed at her as she drove. If she hadn't texted Violet, her friend wouldn't have been out driving so early, and none of this would have happened.

The scene of the accident was impossible to miss. Flashing lights, two police cruisers, an ambulance, and Violet's car with its crumpled hood were all pulled up along the opposite side of the road she was driving on.

She went a little further and pulled as far onto the shoulder as she could, leaving her hazards on as she got out of the truck. After looking both ways to make sure she wouldn't be the next victim in a car accident, she rushed across to the other side. She recognized Officer Hendricks talking to Violet by her car and hurried over to them.

He gave her a grim nod as she approached. Her friend was wiping her eyes with a tissue, and she looked more broken than Flora had ever seen her.

"Thank you for coming, Ms. Abner," Officer Hendricks said. "I think it might be best if you keep your friend company for a while. This has been very traumatic experience for her."

Of course it has, Flora thought. Accident or not, she was responsible for someone's death.

"I'll stay with her for as long as she needs me too," she promised. "Violet, are you hurt?"

Her friend shook her head. "I'm fine. But that poor man…"

"It wasn't your fault," Officer Hendricks told her kindly. "There was no avoiding it, and your presence here means we have some leads to go on, at least. If no one was on the road when it happened, our chances of finding the culprit would not be good. Remember what the paramedics told you, though. You should get a medical checkup today, if possible. You might not feel any injuries right now, but you will be sore later. This was a high-speed collision, and invisible injuries such as whiplash are highly likely."

A sedan came up the road from town, slowing to a crawl as it went by them. Flora saw Natalie peering over at them through the sedan's window. She had no idea where the other woman had been so early, but her neighbor's eyes widened when she saw Flora. Flora did her best to ignore her as Natalie slowly continued on her way, focusing instead on what Officer Hendricks had said.

"I'm confused. I thought Violet –" She broke off, not wanting to say something that might upset her friend further, even if it was the truth.

"I will let her tell you the full story when she's ready, but to clarify, the victim was already deceased when her car struck him. We have reason to believe it was a homicide, and are going to be proceeding as such, but your friend is not in any legal trouble at the moment."

That was a relief, but also extremely confusing. Last time Flora checked, dead men didn't spend a lot of time walking down the road.

"Can we go?" Violet asked, her voice breaking. Her eyes darted toward something in front of her car, and when Flora followed her gaze, she saw a body covered in a white sheet. Debris from Violet's car was scattered down the road.

"Of course," Flora said. "Do you need anything out of your car?"

Violet grabbed her keys and her purse, and Officer Hendricks nodded in farewell as they walked past him. Flora did her best to focus on her friend's well-being for now. Questions and answers could come later. A man might still be dead, but she felt deeply relieved that Violet hadn't been responsible for it – no matter how puzzling the explanation was.

She made sure Violet was buckled into the passenger seat before she put her truck back into drive and turned off the hazards. "Do you want to go home?"

Violet shook her head. "Can we go to your house? I don't want my neighbors to see this and wonder what's going on. I need some time to calm down first."

"Of course," Flora said. She pulled further down the road so she could use someone's driveway to turn around, then headed back past the accident scene and toward home.

"You should call Grady," Violet said unexpectedly as Flora turned onto her street.

"He's at work," Flora said. "If you want him to come over –"

"It's not that. The person… the person I hit was Mr. Brant."

Grady's boss. Flora inhaled sharply, her fingers tightening around the steering wheel. She remembered Grady telling her earlier that his boss wasn't in yet.

"Are you sure?"

Violet nodded. "It was him. I thought there might still be a chance he was alive, so as soon as my car stopped I got out to check." She took a deep breath. "I was driving to your place, and there was this rusty old red truck ahead of me, and the tailgate kept rattling every time it went over a bump, and then suddenly the tailgate fell open and his body fell out. It happened right in front of me. There wasn't a chance for me to stop, and I must've been going at least sixty miles an hour. The truck sped off as soon as it happened. It was *horrible*. The paramedic said he'd already been dead for a while but before they got there, I thought I might've killed him."

Mr. Brant was dead. It felt unreal to Flora. She hadn't known the elderly man well, but she had seen him almost every single time she went to the hardware store. He had been half deaf, and she'd had to shout her greetings at him, and he was little grumpy sometimes, but he had been a fixture here in Warbler. He had a daughter who lived in town, for goodness sakes.

And he had been Grady's boss for years. Grady practically ran the hardware store, since Mr. Brant didn't do much more than work the register, but she had to wonder what would happen to the place without him.

Flora pulled into her driveway and shut the truck's engine off. Violet wiped her eyes again, then in a tearful voice said, "I'm so sorry. I forgot the drinks in my car. I think they spilled when I hit him."

"Don't worry about that," Flora said. "I'll make us some coffee, if you want. Come on, let's go in."

Amaretto greeted them at the door. She had to shoo the cat away so she didn't dart out, and then shut the door quickly behind them. She led Violet over to the couch and made sure the woman was comfortable, then sat down in the armchair kiddy-corner from her.

"What do you need? Can I get you anything to eat or drink? Do you want me to call anyone else for you?"

"Just water," Violet said. "And no, I'll tell Sydney about it later, but right now I just want some time to think."

Flora nodded her understanding and with a single pat on her friend's shoulder, she got up and went into the kitchen. Fetching a glass from the cupboard, she walked over to the sink and turned it on, but nothing happened. With a groan, she remembered that she had shut the water off.

She didn't have any water bottles — she used a reusable one when she was working in the yard. There was some lemonade in the fridge, along with some juice, milk, and a couple of cans of the hard cider she liked, but Violet had asked for water. She hesitated, then put the glass down and hurried to the basement.

After turning the water back on, she rushed upstairs, filled the glass, then ran as fast as she could back down into the basement to turn it off again. She knew she had made more of a mess in the bathroom, but she wasn't about to tell Violet what she had done and make her feel worse.

If her friend wanted a glass of water right now, she would get one. It might be a small thing, but it was all Flora could do.

CHAPTER THREE

Once Violet had her water, Flora returned to the kitchen to try calling the hardware store, but no one answered. Since it was the store phone, she didn't leave a voice message. Instead, she stood by the kitchen window and fretted. Grady had known Mr. Brant for years. She didn't know how close they were, but she was sure he was going to take this news hard. And not just because someone he knew was dead – he very well could lose his job because of this.

She decided to try calling again in half an hour. When she returned to the living room, Violet had shifted on the couch so she could look over the back of it, and was gazing out the window. Flora followed her gaze and saw that a little sparrow was hopping around on the damp towels she had put out earlier.

She made a face. She was going to have to wash those too, but she let it be for now. Amaretto was gazing out the window with an even more rapt expression than Violet's, and Flora spared a moment to be glad for the bird that she didn't allow her cat outside. Amaretto might be a spoiled fluffy Persian with a slightly squished face, but she had all of the same hunting instincts any cat did.

"This doesn't feel real," Violet said quietly as Flora sat back down in the armchair. "How could something like this happen? Who would kill him? He was just an old man."

"I don't know," Flora said. "You didn't recognize the truck?"

Her friend shook her head. "I didn't get the license plate number either. I'd probably recognize it if I saw it again, though. I hope they find whoever was driving it. They were moving his body like it was a bag of gravel."

Flora didn't know what to say to that. She felt very out of her depth. The leaking pipe in the bathroom seemed like such a small thing now, and it seemed absurd how upset she was about it that morning.

"Someone's coming," Violet said.

Flora looked out the window again. Sure enough,

a pickup truck was pulling up in front of her house. It slowed to turn op her driveway, and she recognized it immediately as Grady's. It was brown and old and a little rusty, and she worried that the sight of it might remind her friend of the red pickup truck she'd seen and upset her more, but Violet just sniffed and said, "I didn't know you'd managed to get in touch with him."

"I didn't," Flora said as she stood up. "The police must have contacted him. I'm going to go talk to him. Will you be all right in here?"

"Yeah. But if he wants to come in, that's fine. He knew Mr. Brant a lot better than either of us did."

She slipped the easy to put on boots she kept by the front door onto her feet and stepped onto the porch just as Grady was getting out of his truck.

"Sorry I didn't call," he said as he approached her. He looked a little dazed. "I got a call from the police at the hardware store. Mr. Brant passed away."

"I know," she said, hurrying forward to pull him into a hug. "I called the hardware store a few minutes ago to tell you."

He squeezed her back, then pulled away, looking at her in confusion. "How did *you* learn about it so quickly?"

She grimaced. "It's a complicated story. Do you

want to come in? Violet is here. I'm not sure if she'll want to talk about it, but we can step into the kitchen so I can explain."

He nodded, still looking puzzled, and followed her into the house. For once, Amaretto didn't greet her at the door. A glance into the living room showed her that the cat was sprawled across Violet's lap. Flora and Grady took their shoes off, then entered the living room. Violet gave Grady a melancholy nod in greeting.

"Violet, do you mind if I tell Grady what happened? We'll go into the kitchen, so we won't disturb you and Amaretto."

"Yeah, he deserves to know," Violet said. "You can tell him. I just don't want to talk about it anymore right now."

"I understand," Flora assured her.

Grady followed her into the kitchen. She reached for the cupboard to get herself a glass of water, then remembered that the water was off, so she took the lemonade out of the fridge instead. She shot a questioning glance to Grady, who nodded, so she poured him a glass as well, then sat at the kitchen table with him. Then, taking a deep breath, she told him the story Violet had told her. It was still confusing, and she had a lot of questions about what had happened, but at least she could give him some answers.

When she was done, his brows were drawn together and he was slowly turning his glass of lemonade around in his hands.

"So what you're saying is, someone killed him before Violet hit him with her car?"

"That's what both Violet and Officer Hendricks said," she told him, keeping her voice quiet so Violet wouldn't be able to overhear them. "I know how strange it sounds, but it's what happened. Violet said the paramedics told her Mr. Brant had already been deceased for a while before the car accident, and since this happened so early in the morning, I'm guessing that means he died sometime last night."

"And they don't have any idea who did it?"

She shook her head. "I don't think they have any leads other than that old, rusty, red pickup truck Violet saw. Do you recognize the description?"

He snorted. "That's half the trucks in Warbler."

She gave a small smile. "True." The expression faded quickly. "I'm sorry, Grady. You've known him for years. This has to be a shock."

"I was so sure I was mishearing the police at first, when they called. They asked me a few questions over the phone, like when I last saw him and if he had mentioned that he had any plans the night before. When I got done talking with them, I decided to close the store for the day and come over here to let you know. Maybe I should have called ahead first. I wasn't thinking clearly."

"It's fine," she said. "You're always welcome here. Do you know what's going to happen to the store now?"

He shook his head. "I'm guessing his daughter might get it. I don't think he has any other family to leave it to. I'll wait until next week and then I'll try to talk to her about it, see if she wants me to keep it running or what. I'd like to wait more than a few days, but if I'm going to need to get a new job, I need to know sooner rather than later."

"I feel terrible for her," she said. She had met Mr. Brant's daughter a few times, and while she didn't like the other woman – Flora had started off suspecting her of murder and that sort of thing didn't really go away – someone getting a call that their parent had passed away was always going to be a gut-wrenching experience. "Did he have any enemies? I mean, I'm sure you probably told the police already, I just can't wrap my mind around who would want to kill him."

"I'm not very comfortable with speaking ill of the

dead, but Mr. Brant wasn't easy to get along with all the time. I know he rented the upper story of his house to someone he frequently got into arguments with, and just yesterday, he banned one of our regulars from the store for having an unpaid tab. The two of them spent a good half an hour arguing back and forth."

"That happened yesterday? Who was it?"

"Ned Hansen. He runs a business painting house interiors for people. I already told the police about it, so I guess they'll be looking into him. I think his tenant's name was Levi, but I never met him. Only saw him watching me through a window once while I was mowing the lawn for Mr. Brant."

"Did he have a busy social life?" Flora asked. "Where would he have gone after you closed yesterday?"

Grady frowned, thinking. "He almost always stopped by that little diner on the way out of town before going home. He'd usually eat dinner there. I don't think he would've gone anywhere else."

Flora sipped her lemonade, thinking. Whoever killed Mr. Brant had to have run into him between when the hardware store closed yesterday and when he got home. That didn't help much — it was a small town and Mr. Brant was a lifelong resident, so a lot of people probably knew his schedule. If only they knew more about that red truck. Whoever was driving it was involved in Mr. Brant's death, even if they didn't kill him with their own two hands.

The only two people who might be able to answer more of her questions deserved some time to process what had happened, though. She had her own emotions to figure out. She hadn't known him well, but he hadn't been a stranger to her either. It didn't seem real yet that she would never again walk into the hardware store to hear him mumble a greeting at her. Even if Grady was able to keep working at the hardware store, it would never be the same.

CHAPTER FOUR

The three of them spent a mournful afternoon at Flora's house until Violet announced she was ready to go home. Grady decided to head back to his trailer as well, and get a head start on finding a potential new job in case the hardware store closed down for good. Despite her objections, he promised to come over the next day to help her with the pipe in the bathroom. He wanted to keep busy, and said he would probably rather spend the day with her than spend it alone doing nothing. She didn't object too much, since she *did* need running water in her house.

She was reluctant to leave Violet alone in her apartment, but her friend promised she would be fine, and pointed out that even though she didn't have a car, she could walk to the grocery store if she needed anything, and could always call Flora if she ended up needing a ride somewhere.

The next morning, Flora drank juice when she woke up instead of coffee, since she didn't want to risk turning the water on to fill the coffee pot, and wondered if Violet would let her take a shower at the apartment if she and Grady didn't manage to get the leaky pipe fixed today. She didn't know much about plumbing, and had no idea how big of a job it was going to be.

He picked her up around ten, two coffees from Violet Delights in his truck's cupholders.

"Is Violet back at work?" she asked as she slid into the passenger seat and he backed the truck out of the driveway.

"No, her employees are running the place," he said. "It was weird stopping in and not seeing her there."

"I bet. I could probably count on one hand the number of times I've gone there when she wasn't working. Thanks for the coffee, by the way. I needed the caffeine."

They rode mostly in silence as Grady drove them to the next town over. He had left the supplies he was going to bring to her house at the hardware store in his hurry to leave yesterday, he didn't seem comfortable with the idea of opening the store even just temporarily to pick up the supplies.

He knew exactly what they needed to get, and it didn't take long to gather up a length of copper pipe, two new joints, one for the corroded joint and the other to join the new pipe to the old one, and a tool to cut the pipes. He seemed optimistic that the job would only take a few minutes, and she tried not to show how skeptical she was. It wasn't that she didn't trust him. It was just that, in her experience, if something *could* go wrong, it would.

She checked in with a quick text message to Violet as they drove back to Warbler. Her friend responded, saying she was doing all right and she planned to be back at work the next day. When Flora asked if she needed anything, and offered to stop at a store for her since she and Grady were already out, Violet turned her down, claiming she just wanted to be alone right now. Flora didn't push her, but she was worried. Even though what happened to Mr. Brant wasn't her friend's fault, she knew Violet was taking it personally.

"I hope the police catch whoever killed him soon," she said. "Have you gotten any updates from the police?"

"No. I was thinking, though, maybe we should

stop by his house and let his tenant know what happened. I don't know if the lease was official, and the police might not have known to tell him. I doubt his daughter is in any condition to remember, either."

"I don't mind stopping," she said.

Grady nodded and when they got to town, he turned the opposite direction they would normally take to her house. Mr. Brant lived in a two-story house not far from the center of town. It was an older house, but seemed well-maintained. She realized, a little belatedly, that she had never seen whatever car Mr. Brant drove parked at the hardware store. There was an antique four-door car sitting in the driveway, but it didn't look like it was driven often. He must have walked to work. A second car, a newer model but a lot more beat up, was sitting next to it.

"It looks like he's home," Grady said. "Do you want to wait in here?"

She shook her head. "No, I'll go up," she said. "I know it's not our responsibility to figure out what happened, but you *did* say he argued with his tenant a lot. I'd like to get a feel for the guy myself, if you don't mind."

They made their way up to the front door together. Grady raised his fist to knock, then frowned and led Flora around to the side instead. She saw a set of rickety wooden steps leading up to an entrance on the second level.

"I doubt he'd answer if someone was knocking on Mr. Brant's door," Grady explained as they climbed the steps. "I forgot he has his own entrance."

They crowded into the little landing at the top of the stairway, and he knocked on the door. It took a moment, but before too long, someone pulled it open. A young man who looked to be in his late teens or early twenties blinked out at them through the screen door. He looked like he had just woken up, even though it was nearly noon.

"Yeah?"

"Hey," Grady said. "I don't know if you remember me. I work for Mr. Brant and helped him with the yard sometimes. My name's Grady."

"Yeah, I saw you working out there this summer. What's up?"

Grady took a deep breath. "I thought I should let you know, Mr. Brant was murdered either early yesterday morning or sometime during the night."

The young man frowned. "Murdered? What happened?"

"No one's sure yet," Flora chimed in. "Did you happen hear anything? A struggle, maybe? Did he have any guests over?"

"What, are you some sort of police detective? I didn't hear anything. I work the night shift and I sleep during the day, so depending on when it happened I was probably either asleep or gone. What's his daughter going to do with the house now that he's gone?"

"I haven't spoken to her yet," Grady said. "You might want to get information about your lease together, though. I can ask if I talk to her before you do. What's your name, again?"

"Levi Holland," he replied. "If you do talk to her, let her know I want to keep renting this place. It's going to take me forever to find somewhere else to live that charges me as little as he did. I'm not above forcing her to evict me if she tries to be unfair about it. Is that all you needed?"

A little taken aback at his brusque behavior, she exchanged a glance with Grady.

"Yeah," Grady said. "That was all."

Levi shut the door in their faces. A little irritated at the rudeness, Flora followed Grady back down the stairs. They got into his truck.

"Well, he certainly didn't seem too bothered that his landlord was murdered," she muttered.

"I told you they didn't get along," he said. "At

least he knows, now. You want to go anywhere else, or just home?"

"You said he normally got dinner at the diner, right?" she asked. "Would you mind swinging by there? We could get some food to take home for lunch, and also ask around and see if he ever came in that night."

He nodded and pulled out of the driveway, heading for their next destination.

CHAPTER FIVE

Flora had only been to the little diner on the outskirts of town once before, when she first moved to Warbler. The heavy, greasy food wasn't to her personal tastes, though it wasn't bad for what it was. She much preferred the sandwich shop, with its offering of fresh ingredients and constantly changing menu. She was perfectly content with getting food from the diner for lunch, though, and there was something to be said about the cozy, welcoming, small-town feel the diner enveloped her in as soon as she and Grady stepped through the doors.

It was a small restaurant, with only a handful of tables and some stools at the counter. She had seen the parking lot absolutely packed on Friday nights, after the local high school's football games, but today business seemed to be slow. Only one table was taken when they walked in, and two people were sitting at the counter. A friendly, middle-aged waitress bustled over as soon as they were through the door.

"Hi, dears. Are you eating here? If so, take any table that catches your eye."

"Actually, we were hoping to get some food to go," Flora said.

"Well, come on up to the register and I'll get your order in. Do you know what you want?"

Flora let Grady order first, while she eyed the menu. The chalkboard had the most interesting items, listing *Bleu Cheese Burger, Asian Fusion Salad, Chicken Dumpling Soup,* and *Deep-Fried Cheesecake.* She ended up getting the bleu cheese burger and deep-fried mushrooms. She knew the heavy meal wouldn't make her feel too good, but it sounded like the perfect comfort food for what had ended up being a pretty bad weekend.

She and Grady held a silent argument over who would pay, but she made sure she won it, considering that Grady might be out of a job unexpectedly. As she handed her card over to the woman, she said, "I know this is a longshot, but would you happen to remember if Mr. Brant came in here two nights ago?"

The woman faltered as she slid the card through the card reader.

"I wasn't working that night. I'd have to go get Patrick for you. I heard what happened to him. Friends of his, are you?"

"Yes," Grady said. "I worked for him for nearly a decade."

"Then you have my condolences," the woman said. She handed the card back to Flora, along with a receipt for her to sign, then bustled off into the kitchen. A moment later, a grizzled man with graying hair came out, wiping freshly washed hands on his apron.

"Angie said you want to talk to me?"

"I was wondering if Mr. Brant came in here two nights ago," Flora said. "I know he was a regular here."

The man eyed them uncertainly.

"What's it to you? I know you aren't investigators. I recognize *him* from the hardware store —" He jabbed his thumb at Grady, "and I don't think you're even a local."

"Just asking around," Grady said. "Trying to piece together what happened."

The man sighed. "Well, he did come in here, to answer your question. Stopped in at seven-thirty, just like he always does. Ordered his usual – a chicken pot pie and a slice of deep-fried cheesecake, before you ask. Nothing seemed off. I already had the police in here asking questions, and I don't have anything to tell you that I didn't tell them."

"Do you happen to remember who else was there that evening?" Flora asked. "Anyone driving a red truck, maybe? It would have been old and rusty."

He frowned. "Sounds like Ned's truck. He only lives a street away, leaves his truck in my parking lot sometimes if he's had more than a few beers."

"Ned Hansen?" Grady asks.

"Of course Ned Hansen, I don't know any other Ned's in town, do you? What's he got to do with this?"

"We're just trying to figure out who might own a truck of that description," Flora said. "I'm Flora by the way. Flora Abner. You're right, I'm new here – I moved here at the beginning of summer."

"Patrick Ford," he said, shaking her hand with some reluctance. "Haven't seen you in here much. There something wrong with my food?"

"Not at all," Flora said. "I'll have to stop in more often." She didn't want to mention that she thought the food was unhealthy – even though she didn't mean that in a bad way, since sometimes greasy diner food was exactly what someone wanted to eat – since she had a feeling he would take offense to it.

"Yeah, well, come in on a game night, and you'll get a free slice of pie if the home team wins. Now, if you want your order, I've got to get back to the kitchen."

He nodded to Grady and went back into the kitchen. Flora exchanged a look with Grady, and he shrugged. There was a gleam in his eye though, and she knew that like her, he was thinking of Ned Hansen. Was that rusty red truck his?

Angie came out with their food in a to-go bag a few minutes later. She bade them a good day as they left, and Flora and Grady got into his truck.

"What now?" she asked.

"Better go eat before this gets cold," he said. "Unless you want to swing by Ned's place and see if that truck's in his driveway."

"You know I do," she said, buckling up. "Do you know where he lives?"

Grady nodded. "He orders paint in bulk, and I've delivered them to him a couple of times. I know he has a big, white work van, but I don't remember what his personal vehicle looks like."

"Well, if it's in the driveway, I'll take a picture and send it to Violet to see if she recognizes it."

She had her fingers crossed that it would be there. Officer Hendricks might not be thrilled about her doing her own investigation, but if she and Grady managed to find the break in the case they needed, he probably wouldn't complain too much.

Sure enough, Ned's house was only a street away from the diner. Grady slowed as he approached it, but the only vehicle they could see in the driveway was a white work van with Ned's phone number and the name of his business on the side. There was no garage, just a shed which didn't look big enough for a pickup truck to park in. A man was outside, taking things out of the van. He looked over his shoulder as Grady drove by, then did a double take and waved Grady down. Grady pulled over, rolling down his window.

"Ned," he said with a nod of greeting. He seemed utterly calm, like they hadn't just been practically stalking the guy. "What do you need?"

"I was hoping you'd let me put another paint order in at the hardware store. I can pay you half of what I owe now, plus half of what the new order will be. I'll get the rest to you after I'm done with this next job. Your paint prices are better than anyone else's, and I don't want to have to go out of town to get supplies."

"The hardware store is closed," Grady said. "Did you hear about what happened to Mr. Brant?"

Ned grimaced. "Saw a post about it online this morning. What a bummer. It came at a bad time, too. How long do you think the store will be closed?"

"Dunno," Grady said. "Could be a few days, could be forever."

Ned heaved a sigh and ran his hand through his short hair. "Well, that's terrible news, Grady. If that place closes for good, I'm going to have to up my prices again, and my customers aren't going to be pleased. I'm already having some cashflow issues. On top of all that, my truck got stolen, so I'm stuck driving this van around for all my errands. It's been a bad week, though I guess given what happened to the old man, I could have it worse."

"Your truck was stolen?" Flora asked, unable to keep the curiosity out of her voice.

Net glowered. "Yeah. Went out for dinner and some beers with a friend a couple nights ago, and I left it parked in front of the diner so I could walk home. I've done it a million times before and never had a problem, but when I went to get it yesterday morning, it was gone. You'd never think that sort of thing could happen here, in Warbler."

"Did you file a police report?"

"Of course I did. It might be a beater, but I'm already having money problems. Do I look like I want to buy another truck? I'm hoping some kids just took it on a joyride, and it'll turn up parked along some road somewhere. It's an old, red pickup truck. If you see one sitting around somewhere it doesn't belong, give me a call, won't you?"

"Will do," Grady said.

"And give me a call when you reopen that store. I know the old man banned me, but he's not around anymore and I'd like to work something out with you, Grady. My number's on file."

Grady nodded and rolled up his window. Ned waved as they pulled away.

Flora let out a low whistle. "Well, the mystery deepens. Do you think he was telling the truth about his truck being stolen?"

"I don't know. I guess we'll have to wait and see if it gets found. It all goes back to that truck."

Flora sighed, because he was right. If anything, they only had more questions now.

CHAPTER SIX

Flora was pleasantly surprised by how quickly Grady fixed the leaky pipe in her bathroom. She stood by, watching what he did and handing him tools as he needed them. He explained each step, and she felt like she understood most of it, though she wasn't sure if she would be confident enough to do it completely on her own if the need arose again.

When she turned on the water in the basement and came back upstairs to see the faucet running without a single leak under the sink, she hugged him tightly.

"Thank you so much!" she said. "I owe you... Grady, you should let me pay you."

He rolled his eyes as he put his tools away. "Not going to happen."

She pouted, but didn't push it. Sure, she felt worse

about it now that she knew he might not have a job anymore, but he had never accepted a cent from her. Now that they had been on a few dates and their relationship had been moving into more romantic territory, she had a feeling he would be even less willing to listen to reason when it came to her paying for all of the ways he had helped her with the house.

He stayed at her house for the next few hours, helping her with a few small tasks she wanted to get out of the way. Thanksgiving was getting ever closer, and so was her aunt's visit. She had finally decided to invite the rest of her family as well, but her brother, who lived out of state, couldn't make it, and her parents had reluctantly told her they had already committed to going to her sister's house for Thanksgiving dinner. They invited her, of course, but she had been tied into her aunt's visit for months now, and unfortunately had to face the fact that getting together with her whole family for the holiday just wasn't going to happen.

Grady left later that evening, but not before telling her he was planning on talking to Mr. Brant's daughter the next day. "I don't have her number, but it's on a list at the hardware store, so I'll go there to do it," he said.

"Do you want to go out to eat afterward?" she

asked. "My treat. I'm going to town during the day anyway, to stop in at Violet Delights and see how Violet is doing."

That way, regardless of what news he got from Mr. Brant's daughter, they would have a nice meal together, and if the news was bad news, they could brainstorm about possible jobs for him.

"Sounds good," he said. They kissed before he left, and she waved as he drove away into the darkening evening. Then she went back inside and luxuriated in the simple convenience of running water.

She left for town at eleven the next morning, heading straight to Violet Delights. The street parking in front of it was unusually full, so she ended up parking down the block at the grocery store and walking to the coffee shop instead. After getting her leaky pipe fixed, she was in high spirits, but all of that ended when, just as she was about to go into the coffee shop, something shattered on the window next to her head. She jerked back and stared at the dripping, raw egg on the glass in shock, then whirled around in time to see some older teenagers run away, laughing.

Stunned, and unsure what that was all about, she went inside. She was shocked to see, of all things, what looked like a reporter trying desperately to talk to Violet as she made drinks. Violet was doing her best to ignore her. A couple of middle-aged women were hanging back, huddled together, and talking in lowered voices. Flora side-eyed them as she made her way up to the register. Violet glanced up, and her expression turned to one of relief when she saw Flora. One of her employees, a young woman just out of high school, looked like she was almost in tears as she handed a drink over to a customer.

"Thank goodness you're here," Violet said to Flora. "Everyone's going insane. Are you busy?"

"No?" Flora asked, befuddled.

"Good. Come around the counter and put an apron on. You remember how to work the drip coffee machine right? Mabel needs a break. It's been a horrible morning."

Flora was about to object, since she had to meet Grady in just half an hour, but she glanced at the young employee again and saw that the woman was failing to blink away her tears. Flora was quick to step around the counter and take the apron from her.

"What's going on?" she hissed to Violet as her friend handed her an order slip for a plain black drip coffee. Flora started pouring it. She had learned the basics of working in the coffee shop a few weeks ago, when she spent a few days staying at her friend's apartment and helping her around the shop.

"Somehow, word got out about what happened with me and Mr. Brant," her friend whispered back. "Or a twisted version of it. People think I killed him when I hit him with my car."

Flora looked up again, spotting the reporter, the group of women who were giving them sour looks, and outside, another teen who threw something at the windows. A middle-aged man was watching, but didn't make a move to stop him.

"I need some fresh air," Mabel muttered. Violet nodded, and the employee rushed out from behind the counter, past the women, who glared at her, dodged the reporter, who tried to shove a microphone in her face, and hurried outside.

"They're trying to get a story about why the police let me go free after I killed a man with my car," Violet muttered. "It's horrible. I'm tempted to close the coffee shop down early today. I just don't want –" She broke off and stared out the window with an expression of horror. Flora followed her gaze, and saw that someone had thrown a rotten piece of fruit at Mabel. She could hear the laughter of the teens even through the glass wall of windows.

Violet stalked out from behind the counter,

yanked the door open, and pulled her employee back inside. Then she rounded on everyone else.

"Everyone, out," she snapped. "If you haven't got your coffee yet, you'll be refunded, but we're closed as of right now."

It was a chaotic few minutes as people argued and shouted, either questions about Mr. Brant's death or complaints about not getting their order, but before too long, Violet managed to empty the coffee shop. Then it was just her, Mabel, and Flora. Flora wetted a rag and brought it to the young woman so she could clean up. Mabel was crying, and Flora felt sick at the cruelty she had seen today.

"I'm so sorry," Violet told her employee. "I didn't expect things to go that far. Why don't you go home? You'll still get paid for today. I need to think about what I'm going to do." Her expression hardened. "I can deal with them being rude to me, but if they're attacking my employees, we're going to have problems."

CHAPTER SEVEN

Violet walked Mabel out to her car in the small lot behind the coffee store. Once she was safely on her way home, Flora helped her tidy up the coffee shop and close for the day. She had never seen her friend so angry before.

"I'm supposed to meet Grady soon for lunch. I'm actually going to be a little late. Do you want to come with us?" Flora asked.

Violet let out a breath. "Yeah. I think that's just what I need. I won't be interrupting a date, will I?"

"No, not really. He's supposed to be talking to Mr. Brant's daughter right now, to see what she wants to do with the hardware store in the long run. I offered to take him out afterward so we could talk about it, whether it's good news or bad news. If it's bad news, maybe you can help us brainstorm what he should do next."

"I really hope she wants to keep it open," Violet said as she grabbed her purse. "That place is a cornerstone of the town. That, the diner, and if I can toot my own horn a little, the coffee shop are all important parts of Warbler."

"Hopefully she'll let him run it," Flora said as they went outside.

"It would be some nice passive income for her, and Grady was already practically running it before Mr. Brant died," Violet agreed.

Flora drove around the block so they could go the opposite way down Main Street. The hardware store wasn't very far from the coffee shop. She parked in the back this time, since she was on the wrong side of the street to park right in front of it, and the two of them got out and walked around to the front. She paused for a moment to look at the small collection of flowers and handwritten cards that were sitting under one of the windows, a memorial for Mr. Brant.

The sign on the hardware store's door read *Closed*, but when she pushed it, it opened easily. Both Grady and Phoebe, Mr. Brant's daughter, looked around when she and Violet came in.

"Sorry for interrupting," Flora said. "Should we

wait outside?"

"No, we're just about done," Grady said.

"Hi, Flora," Phoebe said. "And Violet, right?"

Violet nodded. "I'm sorry for your loss," Flora said.

Phoebe bowed her head. "Thank you. It's been… difficult. I've had a lot of people come up to me to give me their condolences, people I've never even seen before. I know my dad was a well-known face around town, and a lot of people grew up seeing him behind the cash register whenever they came in here, but it's hard. It made me realize how few people really knew him. He wasn't just the guy who owns the hardware store. He was my dad. He played softball for the local team until his arthritis got too bad, he loved going to the farmer's market every Sunday in the summer, he hated the fact that everything has a touchscreen now, he was allergic to peanuts, and he used to love listening to his record player before he lost his hearing. He wasn't just some sort of… caricature of a grumpy old guy who ran a hardware store."

"I'm sorry," Flora said. "I only knew him through the store like a lot of other people did, but for what it's worth, I'm going to miss him. It was obvious that he loved you deeply."

"Thanks," Phoebe said. "I knew he was getting

older, and that he wouldn't be around forever, but it was so sudden. I can hardly believe he's gone. Everything seems to be moving so quickly, too. The funeral's going to be in ten days. I'd like to have it sooner, but since his death is under investigation, the police need to wait until the coroner has finished looking over his body first. You can come if you want. I've already invited Grady, of course. I'm trying to keep it smaller, so only people who actually knew him will be there. I don't want to make a spectacle out of it."

"I'll be there," Flora said.

"So will I," Violet said.

Phoebe held her eye and nodded. Flora guessed she knew the full truth of what had happened, and how it had affected Violet. The police must have told her, and she seemed to feel sympathy towards the other woman more than anything.

Phoebe turned back to Grady. "I'm sorry I don't have better news for you. I'm already going to be handling his entire estate, and I still have to figure out what to do about his house and if I can legally sell it with the tenant in it, or if I want to move into it. The fact that he is renting it to someone makes it harder, because I don't want to live with a housemate, but I don't think I can legally break the lease. I can't handle taking care of the store too. I don't want to see it shut down – I know my father wouldn't want that – but I'm already at the end of the rope. You know more about what this place is worth than I do. Take a look at the finances, put an offer together, and I'll have my lawyer look over it. Unless it's an extremely low-ball offer, I'll accept it. I just want to know this place is in good hands, and if anyone deserves to run it, it's you. I don't need an answer now, but could you let me know what decision you're leaning toward by the end of the week?"

Grady nodded, though his expression was grim. Phoebe said a quick goodbye to him, Flora, and Violet, then exited the hardware store. Flora raised her eyebrows and watched as the woman walked away down the sidewalk.

"Did she offer to sell the store to you?"

Grady sighed. "Yeah, but there is no way I could afford it. She's giving me the first chance to buy it, but if I'm not interested, she's going to list it for sale. One of those big chains will probably snatch it up."

"You can't let that happen," Violet said, horrified. "There are so many family-owned businesses in Warbler, and it's one of the things that makes the town so charming. If we start getting chain stores in here, everything is going to change."

"You can't wring money out of a stone, and

there's no way I can afford what this place is worth. Trust me, I'd like to." He paused and looked around, taking in the store he had worked at for nearly ten years, which he had practically been running by the end. "Owning this place would be a dream. There's so many things Mr. Brant never wanted to update or change, and it needs a good cleaning and some organization, but I can see what it has the potential to be." He shrugged. "It just a dream, though. I'll probably be able to keep working here until it sells. Maybe whoever buys it will want to keep me on as manager."

"This day sucks," Violet decided. "Flora said you two were going to grab lunch. Mind if I tag along?"

"Of course not," he said. He paused, eyeing them, as if just realizing that they were both here. "Why aren't you at work, anyway? I thought you were going back in today."

Violet gave him an icy smile. "Oh, I was there all morning, until some jerk threw a rotten fruit at one of my employees. I kicked everyone out and shut the coffee shop down for the day. I don't know yet if I'm going to reopen tomorrow. Anyway, I'm starving. I was going to send Mabel to pick up sandwiches for lunch, but I didn't get around to it before everything happened. Let's head out. We can talk more once we have some food in our hands."

"Should we call Sydney too?" Grady asked, grabbing his keys. "He called me last night to see if I would be free today. He has the day off."

Violet glanced at Flora, who shrugged. She was happy to have Sydney tag along too. Violet nodded. "Sure. I called him to tell him what happened with Mr. Brant, but I haven't seen him yet after the accident. It'll be good to have all four of us together again."

"Sounds like we have a lot to talk about," Flora said. "Considering... well, everything that happened this morning, it might be better if we grab the food to go and head to my house."

Violet winced. "You're right. If one of you wants to call in the sandwich order, I'll give Sydney a call and see if he wants to meet us at Flora's house. He always gets the Italian club sandwich, so just get one of those for him, and if he doesn't end up coming, I'll take it home and eat it for lunch tomorrow."

Flora nodded and grabbed her cell phone to make the sandwich order. This wasn't how she expected the day to turn out, but at least she and her friends would get a chance to brainstorm together. She was sure that, between the four of them, they would be able to come up with a way to help fix Violet's reputation, and to help Grady keep the hardware store.

CHAPTER EIGHT

She and Violet stopped by the sandwich shop to pick up the order, while Grady swung by Sydney's house to carpool with him. They arrived at Flora's home at almost the same time, and walked in together. Amaretto was happy to see so many people she knew, and spent a content few minutes being petted by the others while Flora got dishes and silverware out for them in the kitchen.

They sat down at her small kitchen table, which was just big enough for the four of them, and dug into their food, taking turns to update Sydney on everything that had happened that morning. He and Violet had been dating casually for a couple of months now, so it was understandable when he focused on her problems first.

"That's unbelievable," he said, aghast, when he heard about the people throwing eggs at her store, and how someone had assaulted Mabel. "How did they even know you were involved in the accident? Whoever started spreading that rumor obviously didn't have the full story. You had nothing to do with his death."

"It has to be someone who drove past while the police were at the accident scene," Violet said. "The three of you are the only ones who I told about what happened, and I know you wouldn't have spread that sort of rumor around, so unless there is a leak in the police department, someone who either didn't have all the information or has it out for me, the only other option I can think of was a passerby who saw the accident scene but didn't have the full story."

Slowly, Flora put her sandwich down. "Natalie."

Grady raised his eyebrows. "Your neighbor?"

She nodded. "She drove past while I was at the scene of the accident to pick Violet up. I saw her slow down to look at it. Mr. Brant's body was covered, but if she saw his death in a post online, she might have put two and two together."

"This is your neighbor who has it out for you, right?" Violet asked.

"Things are… civil between us, but she's not my

biggest fan. I don't blame her; I *have* been involved in two incidents that led to the police coming to her house. Neither were my fault, exactly, but I don't blame her for not wanting to have anything to do with me. If she is spreading rumor like this about one of my best friends on purpose, though, I'm going to have to have words with her."

Violet sighed. "I doubt she's doing it maliciously. I understand how it looked. Any sane person would assume I hit him after seeing that accident scene. Because I *did*. It's just that he was already dead when it happened. There is no way she could've guessed that part of it. I'm not thrilled that she spread the news around, but she's probably just telling the truth as she understands it."

"That doesn't mean it's okay," Flora said. "Her spreading rumors around led directly to what happened today."

Violet wilted. "I know. It's not fair. Mabel's just a kid, barely out of high school. She didn't deserve that today. I can't keep the coffee shop closed forever, but I think I'm going to wait at least a couple of days before opening it again, and when I do, I'll spend the first shift working by myself until I'm sure there won't be a repeat of today."

"It's not fair for them to run you out of your own

coffee shop when you didn't do anything wrong," Sydney said. "You're going to be losing money every day it's closed."

"I know, but it's the only thing I can think to do. You didn't see them today, Sydney. There was a *news crew* there. I saw some of my regulars looking at me with real hate in their eyes. They think I killed a man with my car and got off Scott free for it. I'd rather lose a few days' worth of business than suffer through all of that again."

"I understand, but it still feels unfair," Sydney said. "I have tomorrow off too, so if you want some company, just let me know."

"I'll have the next few days off as well," Grady said. "Phoebe asked me to reopen the hardware store on Friday. She thinks having it closed for a week is enough time to respect her father's memory, but she doesn't want to lose too much business. She wants the store to be doing well when she sells it."

"Dude, she's offering you a great deal from what Violet and Flora said. You should totally buy that place. You'd love it, and you'd be great at running it." Sydney said.

"I can't afford anything close to a fair price for it," he muttered, picking at his sandwich. "I've got some savings, but it's not much, and Mr. Brant's never paid me much more than minimum wage. As much as I want to buy the store, I don't have a chance at it."

"Why don't you take out a business loan?" Violet suggested. "That's what I did when I opened my coffee shop. I'm sure you would have an even easier time getting approved than I did, since the hardware store is already a profitable business. My loan was more risky, since I was opening a brand-new business, and those aren't usually profitable for a few years, if ever."

"I've never done anything like that before," Grady said. "I wouldn't know where to start."

"I'll help you," Violet said. "It will give me something to do over these next few days. We can put together a plan, and check the rates at the local credit unions. I bet you anything you'd be able to qualify for one. Just think, that place would be *yours*."

Grady hesitated and glanced at Flora. "What do you think?"

"Well, I've never taken out a business loan either, unless you count the loan my aunt gave me. But I think it's a great idea. Like Violet said, it would be low risk. Yeah, you'd have to pay it back, and you already know the hardware store is profitable. It has a great customer base, it's the only hardware store in town, and you know the ins and outs of running it. If you can get approved for a loan to buy it, I think it would be an amazing idea."

He started to look more hopeful, and Flora smiled at the growing excitement in his eyes. "I'll have to figure out how much it's worth. I want to offer her a fair price, but as low as possible. She *did* say she would accept anything that wasn't a complete low-ball offer."

"You've got this," Sydney said, raising a hand to high-five him. "Violet knows what she's talking about. With her help, I'm sure you'll be able to get a loan. And forget about worrying about losing your job. You'll be set for good."

"So, Grady's got to work on buying the hardware store, which is closed until Friday; Violet, you've got the next couple days off; and so do you Sydney. I should keep working on the house, but I can take a day or two off if I want to." Flora smiled slowly. "What do you say we take tomorrow to do something fun? I think we could all use a chance to just relax and enjoy our lives for a little while."

"That sounds good to me," Violet said, while Grady nodded.

Sydney said, "Let's go fishing. It's been forever since I've gone fishing, and the weather has been cooling down, so we won't roast while we're outside."

"I haven't gone fishing since I was a kid," Flora said. "I don't even own a fishing pole."

"I've got extras," Grady said.

"And I know a good place," Sydney said. "What do you guys say? We take a day to go fishing, hang out, and just relax, then we'll get back to solving all our problems?"

Violet grinned, Grady nodded, and Flora smiled. It sounded like a great plan.

CHAPTER NINE

Flora felt a little guilty about taking the next day off. She still had a lot to do around the house. There was wallpaper that needed to be removed, trim that needed to be painted, floors that needed to be redone, not to mention the fact that she still needed to decide whether she was going to update the kitchen and the bathrooms or not before she flipped the house. And that was on top of all of the small stuff that seemed to keep piling up, like the scratches in the staircase banister, the crumbling cement blocks in the basement, and the huge project of cleaning up the overgrown pond in the forest behind her house.

One day wouldn't hurt, though, and she knew that sometimes a mental health day with her friends was just what she needed.

She didn't have a cooler of her own, but Grady brought one over the next morning and they packed bags of ice and cold drinks into it, then spent some time making sandwiches for everyone. Grady had brought a few fishing poles, and Sydney was in charge of bringing the worms, since he could swing by the feed store and get them at a discount. He and Violet arrived while she and Grady were still packing the cooler. They dragged everything out to Flora's truck, since it had more space than Grady's truck or Sydney's sedan. They wanted to ride together, which was good because Sydney was the only one who knew where they were going.

They were about to pull out of the driveway when Grady realized they would need a bucket to put fish in if they wanted to keep any to eat. He and Flora raced out to the shed to find a big, empty orange bucket to take with them. As they returned to the truck, Flora spotted her elderly neighbor, Beth, walking down the road toward her house, with her droopy basset hound named Sammy at her side.

She handed the bucket to Grady to put in the bed of the truck, then walked out to meet her neighbor. It was going to delay them, but it would be rude to just leave without saying hello to her.

"Good morning, dear," Beth said. "When I peeked

out my window and saw the cars at your house so early, it piqued my curiosity. No offense, but you usually aren't such an early riser."

Flora didn't think she slept unusually late. She usually woke up a little after eight, and rarely left her house before nine. Beth was one of those people who was up at five or six every single morning.

"We're going on a fishing trip," she said. "Apparently, the fish bite better in the mornings."

"Oh, Tim loves to go fishing," Beth said. Tim was her husband, an elderly man who was increasingly suffering from memory issues. Flora rarely saw him. "I'll have to go with him sometime soon. He'd be so thrilled to see pictures of whatever you catch."

"I'll remember to take some," Flora said. She stooped down to pet Sammy before straightening up again. "Sorry to chat and run, but I don't want to keep everyone else waiting."

"No, you go on ahead, dear," Beth said. "It's just... I happened to recognize that friend of yours. Violet's her name, right?"

Flora paused in the middle of turning to go back to the truck. "Yes?"

"Well, I don't know if you're aware, but I heard from a friend of mine that she was involved in a hit-and-run accident that led to the death of Elliot Brant. I thought I ought to let you know. I understand people make poor choices sometimes, but forgiveness only goes so far when a life was lost, don't you agree?"

Flora crossed her arms. "Beth, I don't know what you've heard, but Violet did not kill Mr. Brant."

"Are you sure?" Beth asked. "Because Natalie told me –"

"I *knew* it was her," Flora muttered. "Look, I know what she *thinks* she saw, but it's more complicated than that. Yes, Violet did hit Mr. Brant's body, but he was already dead. The police are treating it as a homicide investigation, and Violet is not under suspicion. I talked to Officer Hendricks myself at the scene of the accident, and he confirmed that the paramedics said Mr. Brant had been deceased for a while prior to the accident. I was *there*. I know Natalie drove past and saw us, but I was there, talking with both of them, and I saw everything firsthand. You can take my word for it, Beth. Violet was *not* responsible for his death."

"Oh my," Beth said. "If you're sure, I'll put the word out with some of my friends. I'm afraid Natalie might have exaggerated things a little. In that case, give your friend my condolences. This can't be an easy time for her."

"I will," Flora said. "You have a good day, Beth.

I'll take some pictures of whatever we catch to show Tim."

She hurried back to the truck and got into the driver's seat. Sydney directed her to turn away from town, and as she headed down the road, she gave them a brief rundown on her conversation with Beth.

"Thanks for defending me," Violet said. "I wish we could post a news bulletin online or something. But if the police haven't released any of the details of the case, we probably shouldn't do anything drastic. As much as I hate being blamed for something that wasn't my fault, I don't want to say something that will make the case harder for the police to resolve."

"Hopefully everything will get cleared up when they catch the real killer," Flora said.

She followed Sydney's directions, making turns onto increasingly bumpy dirt roads. Some of them didn't even have road signs, and it was only Sydney's assurance that kept her from worrying that she was driving up someone's driveway.

Finally he said, "All right, the next left turn will be a path that leads right to a little clearing by the river. It's a great fishing spot, and it's so far out that it's almost always empty. We should have the place to ourselves. If someone *is* there, I know another spot we can go to."

She hit her blinker and made the turn, slowing down to a crawl. This was hardly a road at all, just two ruts and some overgrown grass. Branches scraped across the side of her truck if she eased it along the path.

They crested a hill, and she heard Sydney heave a sigh of disappointment as a red truck came into view.

"I guess we weren't quick enough to get out here. You can turn around in the field, and I'll direct you to the other spot."

Flora didn't take her foot off of her truck's brake. Violet was staring at the truck like she'd seen a ghost, and Flora couldn't take her eyes off it either as she fully registered the color and condition of it.

It was an old, rusty, red pickup truck. It was covered in dew and fallen leaves, which told her it must have been parked here for a few days.

Flora exchanged a look with Violet, whose eyes were wide.

They had just found Ned Hansen's stolen pickup truck; the same truck Mr. Brant's body had fallen from the morning of the accident.

CHAPTER TEN

None of them were sure what to do at first. Flora was tempted to get out and peek into the truck's windows to see if there was anything incriminating inside, but Violet pointed out that they didn't want to interfere with the police investigation. They tried calling the police station, but they didn't have service this far out, so Sydney had to guide Flora back towards town, since she was hopelessly lost. When they finally got back on the main road, Violet made the call. The officer she spoke to instructed them to wait near an intersection on the main road so he could meet up with them and they could guide him to the truck, since there were a lot of little fishing spots and pull-offs by the river, and it would take him a long time to find the right one on his own, even with Sydney's directions.

After they guided the patrol car to where they found the truck, the officer thanked them and dismissed them, promising to call if he had any other questions.

And that was it. It was made clear they had to leave, and Sydney reluctantly directed them toward the other fishing spot he knew of, with no answers to any of their many questions.

They spent the next few hours chatting about the truck as they fished. It having finally been located could only be a good thing, but they were all impatient to know what would happen next.

It was frustrating to have to wait for answers with everyone else, but there was nothing they could do about it. Flora did her best to focus on the fishing excursion. She took pictures of every fish they caught, but they didn't end up keeping anything, and threw the fish back into the river once they removed the hooks from their mouths.

It was a lot of fun, though it wasn't as relaxing as she had hoped after running across the truck. She knew it was on each of their minds, even if they had agreed to drop the subject.

They went their separate ways after getting back

to Flora's house that afternoon. Violet wanted to get some chores done at her house, and since Sydney had picked her up that morning, he went with her. Grady volunteered to stay with Flora and help her start the long process of removing the wallpaper along the staircase.

"If you have time to meet tomorrow, I'll bring over a bunch of papers that I have from my own business loan, and we can start figuring out what all you'll need," Violet told Grady as she and Sydney prepared to leave.

"We can meet at the hardware store," Grady said. "All of the information about the store's finances is there, and I'm sure we'll need that. You want to meet in the morning? Around ten?"

Violet nodded, and Flora agreed to be there too. Sydney had to work, unfortunately, but Flora was sure the three of them could handle it. One way or another, Grady was going to own that hardware store. She was sure of it.

Flora woke the next morning, ready to enjoy the first normal morning she'd had in a long time. She got up and made her coffee, sipping it while Amaretto ate her breakfast. When she showered, she appreciated again how convenient it was to have running water in her house. It was just turning nine by the time she was dressed and ready for the day. She thought about what Beth had said, about her not waking up early, and made a face. She liked the other woman, she really did, but Beth wasn't always the easiest person to get along with. She thought her morning routine was perfectly reasonable. She didn't have anywhere to be super early, so why on earth would she wake up in the wee hours of the morning when she didn't have to? It wasn't as if she slept until noon every day.

She grumbled to herself as she did her breakfast dishes, though she fell silent when her phone rang. The call was from Grady, so she answered it and put it on speakerphone.

"Hey."

"Hey yourself," he replied. "I tried calling Violet, but she didn't answer and her voicemail was full. I need to go mow Mr. Brant's lawn. His daughter asked me to keep it up, and the grass is getting long. I just checked the weather report, and it's supposed to rain for the next couple of days. If I don't get it done now, it's going to have to wait until this weekend. It should only take me about an hour or two, but I probably won't be able to meet at the hardware store until around eleven. Can you let her know?"

"Of course," she said. "I'll send her a text. I know

I've said it a lot, but you really should get a cell phone."

"We'll see. Maybe if I end up buying the hardware store I will."

She said her goodbyes and finished doing her dishes, then sent a text out to Violet to let her know Grady was going to be late. Her friend replied a minute later saying, *I just saw I had a missed call from him. I had my phone on silent, and I've had people leaving nasty messages on my voicemail all morning. Tell him I'm sorry for not answering. 11 is fine.*

She did some laundry while she waited, then started picking at the wallpaper on the stairs again. Her heart wasn't in it, and when her phone rang again almost an hour later, she was glad for the excuse to give up on the job and go answer it.

It was a local number, but not one she recognized. "Hello?"

"It's me," Grady said. "I'm calling from Mr. Brant's house."

"Do something happen?" she asked.

"I noticed one of the curtain rods had been torn down, and when I looked in the window, the place was a mess," he said. "It struck me as odd, so I used my key to get in. The house has been ransacked. The door was locked, and I'm not sure who else he gave a key to, but there *is* a door leading between his part of the house and Levi's, and that wasn't locked. Levi isn't here. I think some of his things are missing. You know I'm not the most comfortable with the police, but do you think I should call them, or let his daughter handle it? My gut says Levi did this and took off rather than wait around for her to evict him."

"Definitely call them," Flora said. "She shouldn't have to deal with more than she already is. I can't believe that guy."

"Me either," Grady said. "Mr. Brant was hardly charging him anything – just a couple hundred bucks a month. He might not have been easy to get along with, but he was doing the kid a favor, and this is how Levi repays him? Anyway, I was hoping you'd have Officer Hendricks' number. He knows me, sort of, and I'd rather talk to him about this than some cop I don't know."

"Of course," she said. "Hold on, let me find it for you."

She rattled off the number and he thanked her before ending the call. She sighed as she put her phone down. Things just kept getting worse and worse, and it all seemed tied to Mr. Brant's death.

As she eyed the remaining wallpaper and tried to

decide if she wanted to spend the next half-hour working on it before she went into town, she realized that Grady must have memorized her cell phone number. The thought was touching. The only number *she* had memorized was 911.

She decided to leave the rest of the wallpaper for now. She wouldn't be able to get much done before she had to leave to meet Grady and Violet anyway. Amaretto was perched on the back of the couch, her tail twitching as she looked out the window, and Flora gave a slow smile.

They had been practicing with the harness for a long time. Amaretto still wasn't a fan of it, but she would at least walk in it sometimes. Flora knew she probably looked like a crazy person, walking her fluffy white cat along the country road, but she was past caring.

"Hey, Amaretto," she cooed, reaching for the harness where it hung on the hook by her jacket. "Do you want to go on a walk?"

CHAPTER ELEVEN

She and Amaretto only made it a hundred yards down the road before the cat found a patch of grass to roll in and refused to move. Eventually, Flora had to pick her up to get her back to the house, but it was still better than their previous record.

"You did great," she said, stroking the cat's spine after she took the harness off. She took the bag of cat treats from her cupboard and gave Amaretto one before grabbing her purse and locking up the house. It was time to go meet Grady and Violet at the hardware store. She hoped things had gone all right when Grady called Officer Hendricks about the break-in at Mr. Brant's house. She really wished he had a cell phone, so she could keep in contact with him more easily.

Grady's truck was already at the hardware store when she arrived, and when she walked in, she saw Violet was there too. Her friend was going to have to get a new car eventually, but for now, she didn't seem to be having too difficult of a time walking everywhere she needed to go. The town was small, and Flora's house was the only place Violet frequented where she would need a ride.

They waved her over when she came in. She eyed the mess of papers on the front counter and let out a low whistle.

"That looks complicated."

Grady pulled a stool up for her, and she put her purse down by her feet as she sat with them. "I second that. Violet made it sound easy."

"It *is*," her friend said. "Well, not easy, but once you know what you're doing, it's not too bad. I think your first step is going to be to get a preapproval for the amount that you're offering to Mr. Brant's daughter. Do you know how much you're going to offer?"

Grady nodded and pushed a pad of paper over to Violet. "I stopped by the library after I left Flora's yesterday and looked up business valuations. I did the math after checking the annual profits of this place, and came up with what I think is a fair offer, if not the highest she could sell it for. It's… a lot."

"It's not too bad," Violet said. "Though, if you're going to be financing all of it, it's going to take a while to pay off."

"I've got roughly two months of savings," Grady said. "It's not going to make a dent in what this place costs."

Violet frowned and started flipping through her papers while Flora turned her attention to Grady. "How did it go with Officer Hendricks?" she asked.

"It went all right. I let him into the house and told him about Levi, then I finished mowing. He was still there when I left. I'm a little surprised he's spending so much time on a B&E. Maybe he thinks it's related to Mr. Brant's death."

"For all we know, it is," she said with a sigh. "Did he say anything about the truck?"

"No. I didn't ask, though. I don't think he likes me that much. He did ask how you were doing, though."

"He's probably surprised *I'm* not the one who found his body," she muttered. "I'm pretty sure he thinks I'm cursed."

"All right," Violet said, looking up from the papers. "So, looking at your finances and what you need the loan to be, and after doing some math with the various interest rates and repayment schedules from *my* business loan – which is a few years old, so I'm sure some things are different now – I think you're going to need to come up with more cash if you want to have a good chance at qualifying for the loan and don't want to pay an arm and a leg every month. Do you have anything you can sell to come up with a bigger down payment?"

"The most expensive thing I own is my truck, and that won't make much of a dent in what this is going to cost either," he said, crossing his arms with a scowl on his face. "Plus, I need to drive. I'm not rich, Violet. I might not be living paycheck to paycheck every month, but it took me years to get there, and I don't have savings like you do. I just don't have the cash."

Violet sighed. "All right, well, there might be other options. You should make an appointment at the credit union and see what they can do. Credit unions usually offer better rates on loans than banks do, and you've already got an account with them."

"What size of a downpayment do you think he should have?" Flora asked.

Violet pointed to a scribbled number on the paper she had been working on. Flora frowned and did some mental math. "I could help," she said slowly.

Grady shook his head. "No. I'm not accepting charity from you."

"You helped me a lot," she said, meeting his gaze. "And you haven't let me pay you a cent. This would be me paying you back for all of the help. If you still feel bad about it, just, like, give me a discount on supplies for the house or something."

Grady's eyes narrowed, then widened slightly. "You could be part owner," he said. "You'd get your discount, you'd get income from this place, and you'd get a say in how the store is run."

Flora's eyes widened. It was a big leap from lending a friend some money out of her personal savings – which, in essence, was just passing on the good deed her aunt had done for her. This was something else, though. This meant setting down roots.

Wasn't that what she had been wanting to do more and more the longer she stayed here? It wasn't as if she would have to live in the area *forever* if she did this. She could always sell her portion of the store later on – maybe even to Grady, so he could be full owner. And in the meantime, it would give her an excuse to stay around Warbler after she flipped her current house. It would also give her a great discount on all the supplies she needed for home improvement, and some passive income. Yes, it would come out of her personal savings, but if she put in some time and effort in to making this hardware store even better than it was now, she would earn all of that back, and she could live off of the money her aunt had lent her in the meantime if she needed to.

"I need to think about this," she said. "I'm not saying no. I like the idea, but it's too big for me to decide in the moment like this. You have until Friday, right?"

It was Tuesday now.

"Yeah, but I'm going to need to talk to my account manager at the credit union and see if I can get a preapproval, before I make the offer to Phoebe."

"Can I think about this until tomorrow?" she asked. "I can give you an answer then."

"Of course. Don't feel like you have to, Flora. Even if this doesn't work out, I'll find something else."

She shook her head. "No, I really am interested. Not just to help you out, though of course I'm happy to do that as well. I want to be self-sufficient. I want to do something I enjoy. I'm not going to be able to make as much money as I need to live comfortably on long term if it takes me two years to flip every house. I was hoping I could start doing two houses at once after I got some experience, but this would be even better. It would be consistent income, and I'd be able to get a hefty discount on the supplies I need."

"If you do this, we'll get everything drawn up legally," he said. "You'd be the official owner of whatever percent you're buying, with all the legal protections just in case things go sour between us later on."

She nodded. Even though she didn't see things ending poorly between her and Grady, it was smart to make sure that they kept the business and personal aspects of their lives separate, at least for now.

Violet looked between them, grinning.

"This is exciting," she said. "If you buy part of the hardware store, does that mean you'll –"

She broke off as the bell over the door jingled. They all looked around to see Ned Hansen come inside.

"Grady," he bit out. "You said you'd call me, man. I need to place a bulk order for paint. I've got half of what I owe you here, in cash. The next closest hardware store wants to charge me almost twenty-five percent higher compared your prices. I need you to help me out."

"I said I'd call you when I reopened the store, but we aren't open," Grady said. "Didn't you see the sign on the door?"

"I saw that you were in here with other people, and I assumed it meant you were open. Come on, I've been buying paint from this place for years. Can't you do me this one favor?"

"We aren't open," Grady repeated. "I'll think about it, and I'll call you Friday."

"I can't wait until Friday," Ned said. He grumbled, ran a hand through his hair, then said, "Look, can we please talk about this? I might be able to figure something out, maybe do some sort of exclusive contract to only buy paint from you in the future. I know I got behind on paying my tab, but I was a good client for years before this. Let's talk about this over food. I'll treat you and your girlfriend to lunch." He glanced at Flora. "Let's have a calm conversation, man-to-man. You know how much paint I buy each month. This would be good for your store, too."

Grady hesitated. Violet started gathering up her papers.

"I need to go anyway. I'm having an employee meeting in an hour, and I need to prepare for it. Give me a call tonight, Flora, if you want to talk about it."

"I will," Flora promised, waving goodbye as Violet left. Ned pulled the door open for her, then raised his eyebrows at Grady.

"Well?"

Grady glanced at Flora. She hesitated. Her heart was pounding – she *knew* that red truck they had found was Ned's, which meant he must have been involved in Mr. Brant's death. A part of her wanted to keep talking to him and get to the bottom of it all, but if they were going to do that, it would be better to do it public place. She gave a small nod.

Grady sighed. "Fine," he said. "We'll talk, but I'm not promising anything. And you're paying, no matter what decision I come to."

"Deal," Ned said. He held the door as Flora and Grady walked out of the store. She tried not to make it obvious that she was staring at him as they walked past.

Were they about to go out to lunch with a murderer?

CHAPTER TWELVE

She and Grady drove to the diner together, following Ned in his work van. He kept glancing at her, worried, and finally she said, "Look, I know we both think he might be responsible for Mr. Brant's death, but he didn't seem like he was about to let this go, and this way we'll be somewhere more public while we're talking to him. If he *is* the killer, maybe he'll let something slip."

"I'm worried he might get violent," Grady said. "You know as well as I do he was the one behind the wheel of that truck with Mr. Brant's body in the back, even if he reported it stolen."

"There will be other people around, so he should be less likely to do anything extreme," she said. "We'll be careful."

They parked in front of the diner a minute later and walked in. Ned held the door open for them, giving them both a tight smile. Flora followed Grady to a table that was right in front of one of the big windows, near the center of the room. She sat next to him and he squeezed her knee as Ned slid into the booth across from them.

"Look at all these familiar faces," a cheerful voice said. Flora turned her head to see Angie approaching them, a pot of coffee in her hand. "Here's your menus. What can I get y'all to drink?"

"Just coffee and water is fine," Flora said.

The others ordered water as well, and then they spent a quiet moment looking over the menus when Angie walked away. Her stomach was twisted into knots, but she thought it would be strange not to order anything. Her eyes landed on the chalkboard above the register, and she read the offerings there. *Shepherd's Pie, Slow-Roasted Chicken with Pearl Onions and Roasted Potatoes, Seasonal Fruit Salad, Deep-Fried Cheesecake (Fried in Peanut Oil)*. It sounded like a heart attack waiting to happen, but she was curious about it, and she didn't think she could stomach a full meal right now.

When Angie came back, she put in her order for a

slice of the deep-fried cheesecake. Grady got a sandwich, and Ned ordered a full burger platter.

"Are you sure neither of you want anything else?" he asked. "Like I said, it's my treat."

"Thanks," Flora said. "But I'm not very hungry, and that cheesecake sounds like it will fill me up."

"Well, as long as you're happy," he said. "Now, Grady, I know I didn't leave things on good terms with Mr. Brant. Like I told him, I had a client back out at the last minute, after I had already put the paint order in with you. I made the mistake of not requiring full payment upfront. I've had a tab with you for years, and it's always paid up in full at the end of every month. This was the only month I've had an issue. I want to get back on track. It would benefit both of us, you *know* I'm one of your biggest customers."

"You didn't get banned because you couldn't pay your tab that month," Grady said. "You got banned because when we said we wouldn't sell you any more paint until the tab was paid off, you started cursing and swearing at us."

Ned flushed. "I know. I'm sorry. Everything just hit all at once. I had to pay my mortgage and that just about cleared out my bank account, I lost that client that backed out, and that was supposed to be my biggest job all month. I had a bunch of useless paint I didn't need, and I had to pay you for it. It was a crappy day, and I shouldn't have taken it out on you. I'm sorry."

"I don't even know what's going to happen to the store," Grady said. "I'm reopening it Friday, but everything is still up in the air. It might get sold to the highest bidder."

"So maybe a contract isn't the way to go. How about I pay an extra ten percent on what I currently owe you? I'd do it just as soon as I get paid for this new job. We've known each other for years, Grady. Can't you do me this one favor? This has been the week from hell for all of us. Between losing that job, and my truck getting stolen, things have been a mess."

"Is your truck still missing?" Flora asked. It was a risky question; she didn't know if Officer Hendricks had told him who found it. To her relief, he shook his head, and didn't seem to think anything of her question.

"It was found dumped out by the river, but the police are holding it for an investigation." His face twisted, but he didn't say what the investigation was for. She wasn't sure if he didn't know, or if he thought bringing up that his truck was involved in Mr. Brant's death wouldn't do him any favors.

The conversation paused while Angie returned with their food. Flora took her fork and tried the deep-fried cheesecake cautiously. It was surprisingly good, the crisp breading pairing nicely with the warm, creamy cheesecake and the tart cherry and rich chocolate syrups drizzled over the top.

She ate another bite, wondering how on earth anyone even deep-fried a slice of cheesecake. It seemed like it would be messy. Did they just toss it in with the fries?

She paused and looked up at the blackboard, where that warning about the cheesecake being fried in peanut oil was written in parentheses. Hadn't Patrick said Mr. Brant ordered the deep-fried cheesecake the night he died? Mr. Brant... who was allergic to peanuts. Maybe she was misremembering what he had said. She glanced at Grady and Ned, who were still arguing about the unpaid paint tab, and excused herself quietly, heading toward the counter to find Angie.

There was no bell at the counter, and Angie didn't reappear while she waited. There was a sign taped up next to the door that led to the kitchen that read

Restrooms this way, and she decided to interpret that as an invitation for her to go back there.

She cautiously opened the kitchen door and stepped inside. Angie was washing dishes at the sink, and Patrick was cutting potatoes on the other side of the kitchen. Angie was the only one who looked up, jumping a little at Flora's unexpected appearance.

"Oh, you can come on in, dear. The bathrooms are through the back, just watch out for the fryer when you go by."

"Thanks," Flora said. "I was actually wondering if I could ask Patrick a question."

Angie frowned. "He's preparing the scalloped potatoes for tonight's menu right now. Maybe I can help you?"

"I don't think so. It's about the night Mr. Brant came in, and you said you weren't here."

"I see." She turned away from Flora and raised her voice. "Patrick! Come talk to Flora, she has a question for you."

Patrick put down the knife and rinsed his hands off in the sink before snagging the hand towel and walking over to her. He looked annoyed at being interrupted.

"Something wrong with your food?"

"No, not at all," Flora said. "The fried cheesecake

is great. I was just wondering, how often do you change the specials?"

"Depends on our ingredients. The main dishes get changed daily, the desserts get changed every Wednesday, so you came just in time to try that cheesecake. Angie's the one who comes up with most of the desserts. I'm more of a meat guy, myself."

"With the cheesecake, you just fry it? In peanut oil?"

He frowned. "That's what the sign says, isn't it?"

"But didn't you say Mr. Brant ordered a slice of the deep-fried cheesecake the day he died?"

Patrick's hands froze where he was drying them off with the hand towel.

"What are you trying to say?"

"I was just wondering if you had a different oil to fry things in for people who are allergic to peanuts."

"Our kitchen's too small for that, dear," Angie called over her shoulder. "It's peanut oil or nothing. Poor Mr. Brant never even got to try the fries. I kept saying we should switch to something else, but Patrick always says nothing tastes quite the same as good old peanut oil."

"So, Mr. Brant came in that night and ordered a slice of deep-fried cheesecake… that was fried in the peanut oil?" Flora asked, her heart beginning to pound in her chest. Patrick slowly dropped his hands to his side, and Angie turned to her with a reassuring expression on her face.

"Oh, no, I'm sure he didn't," she said. "We all know about his allergy. He probably just got a regular slice of cheesecake, no frying needed. If you're worried about it, I'm sure I could look up his order receipt. The specials are extra, so it would be easy to tell."

Without warning, Patrick shoved past her and rushed out of the kitchen. Angie watched him go in confusion, but Flora felt a spark of clarity.

They had been wrong. They had been so, so wrong. Patrick was working here alone the night of Mr. Brant's death. The diner closed at eight, so Mr. Brant had probably been one of his last customers. She was *certain* the warning about peanut oil wasn't on the blackboard the first time she and Grady came in, which meant it hadn't been on the blackboard when Mr. Brant was here either. He would have ordered the deep-fried cheesecake without thinking, and if Patrick was tired after a long day spent working over the stove...

"That doesn't explain the truck," she muttered.

"Are you all right, dear? You look like you've seen a ghost."

Flora shook her head and stumbled out of the kitchen. Ned seemed to have cornered Patrick before he could reach the door, and looked like he was trying to convince him of something. Grady gave her a puzzled look, probably wondering what she had done in the kitchen to send Patrick running out like that. But Flora was staring at Ned as something occurred to her.

He had said he often left his truck parked in the diner's parking lot when he had a few drinks, and he had left his truck there the night Mr. Brant died, only for it to be stolen before he could get it in the morning.

"I don't get it, what's the rush?" Ned was saying. "We've been friends for years, Patrick. I need you to put in a good word for me with Grady. Tell him I'm good for my word."

"I need to get out of here," Patrick said, shoving Ned back.

"What's gotten into you?"

Before things could escalate, Angie came through from the kitchen. "I found it," she announced. "You were right, Flora. He *did* order the deep-fried cheese-cake that night."

Patrick slowly turned to look at her, his face pale.

Grady frowned, but Flora saw his eyes dart to the blackboard and it all seemed to click for him.

"Oh, Patrick, you didn't serve him the deep-fried cheesecake, did you?" Angie asked, pressing her fingers to her lips.

Patrick backed away from Ned, who had broken off from his argument in confusion. "You don't understand. It was an accident. It was late, I wasn't thinking. I wouldn't have forgotten not to give him fries or onion rings or those deep-fried mushrooms, but the cheesecake was new and I didn't even think of it. It was an accident."

"I don't get it," Ned said. "What's going on?"

Grady stood up slowly and came to stand by Flora.

"Mr. Brant was allergic to peanuts," he said.

Ned's brow furrowed. "So? What does this have to do with anything?"

"Patrick, did he die *here*?" Angie asked quietly.

"I found him in the bathroom," Patrick whispered, his eyes wide and red-rimmed. "It was too late. He was already gone. I didn't know what to do."

"You decided to hide his body, and you took Ned's truck to do it, didn't you?" Flora asked.

"You did *what*?" Ned snapped.

"I didn't want to go to prison," Patrick said. "It

was my fault for feeding him that cheesecake, I *knew* he was allergic to peanuts, I just didn't think of it. If I dumped his body somewhere, I thought people would think he just wandered off and dropped dead of a heart attack. But then the truck's tailgate failed and that poor driver behind me hit him, and I knew I had to dump the truck too, if I didn't want it getting back to me. You have to understand, it's not my fault. I didn't mean to kill him."

"You used my truck to hide a body?" Ned asked, grabbing Patrick by the shoulder. "I was questioned by the police for that, man."

Grady hurried forward to pull him away. Patrick backed away from them both, and for a second Flora thought he was going to make a run for it, but then Angie walked over to the diner's phone and picked it up, a sad, stern look on her face.

"I know it was an accident, but you have to face up to what you did," she said. "You sit your butt down in a chair, Patrick. We'll get this all straightened out. And as soon as I get off the phone with the police, I'm dumping all of that peanut oil out back and I'm never touching the stuff again."

EPILOGUE

Flora signed on the dotted line. It had been a busy few weeks, and she hadn't gotten as much done at the house as she would have liked, but the sale of the hardware store moved fast. The day after Patrick's arrest, she and Grady had gone to his credit union together to show them their business plan and see how much of a loan they could offer Grady. He got approved for seventy percent of the offer he wanted to make, and when he took the preapproval letter and the offer to Phoebe, she accepted it.

It took time for all of the papers to transfer the business to get drawn up, but now Flora was officially a thirty-percent owner of the hardware store. She stared at her signature before the lawyer pulled the paper away, and then shook her and Grady's hands.

"Congratulations," he said. "You're all set."

She and Grady exchanged a slightly dazed look. Flora's personal savings had dwindled to almost nothing, but she had the money from her aunt she could fall back on if she needed to, and soon she would have income from the hardware store as well. She was planning on working there a couple of mornings a week for now, but most of her focus would need to remain on her house.

"I can't believe we did that," she said as they walked out onto the sidewalk along Main Street. "We own a hardware store. *You* own a hardware store."

They had already agreed he would do the bulk of the work for the store, and as a consequence, draw the biggest paycheck. It was only fair, since Flora had other things to focus on anyway.

"Everything is going to change," he said, gazing down the street at where the hardware store sat at the end of the block, amazement in his eyes. "I can't believe it's mine."

She squeezed his hand, still feeling more than a little shocked herself.

In time, she might decide to sell her stake in the business, but for now, her ties to Warbler were stronger than ever.

And that didn't feel like a bad thing.

Printed in Great Britain
by Amazon